Fussy Freda

by Julia Jarman and Fred Blunt

There was a girl called Fussy Freda
whose mum and dad tried hard to feed her.

But it didn't matter what they cooked,
Freda only shouted, 'YUK! YUK! YUK! YUK!

I don't like
cabbage,

I don't like
beans,

I don't like
anything

coloured **green.**'

Her mother tried

and tried to feed her,

but **nothing** she cooked suited Freda.

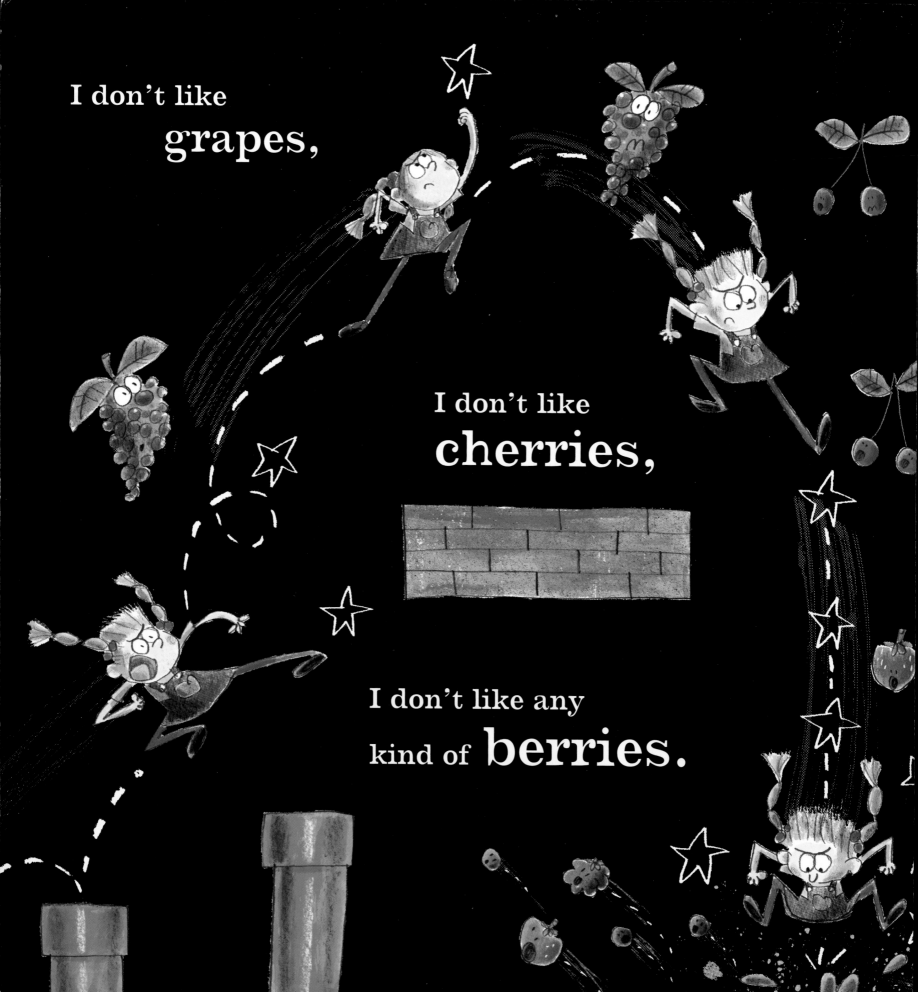

I don't like
grapes,

I don't like
cherries,

I don't like any
kind of **berries.**

Raw or baked or in a stew,

I don't like purple, red or blue!'

Her father tried his best to feed her,
but nothing suited **Fussy Freda**.

He cooked
her **Chinese
crispy duck,**

Grandma said that she would feed her.
'Fish and chips might tempt our Freda.'

The Cod Father

With fingers crossed Mum said, 'Good luck!'
But Freda only shouted, 'YUK!

I don't like **cod.**

I don't like **hake.**

I won't eat **fish,** it makes me **shake.**'

Her aunt and uncle came to stay
with food from their French holiday.

But Freda wouldn't eat or drink.

She refused it all and began to. . .

. . .shrink!

Freda got
shorter

and
shorter

and
shorter!

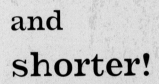

One day Father said, 'Where is our daughter?'

They found her playing in her doll's house,

where Claws the Cat thought he saw a mouse!

Mother cried out, 'That's Freda, Claws!'
But the cat had closed his hungry jaws.

WAS THAT THE END OF
FUSSY FREDA WHOSE PARENTS
TRIED AND TRIED TO FEED HER?

Well, from the cat
There came a shout.

HELP!

'YUK!'

he yowled,

and spat Freda out!

'Give me something to eat,' she said.

'W-what would you like?'
they asked with dread.

'Oh, anything,'
sighed Freda. 'Oh!
I want to eat and I
want to grow!'

She ate **saucy beans**

and **buttered toast.**

She ate **spaghetti,**

she ate a **roast.**

She ate **red cherries**

and **rich brown stew,**

and Freda
grew

and
grew

and

GREW!

And what is more she started to cook –

stir-fries,

sausages

and **crispy duck.**

Pancakes,

pizzas,

pasta bake.

Casseroles

and chocolate cake.

She's writing her very own recipe book,

and she never – well hardly ever – says

HODDER CHILDREN'S BOOKS

First published in Great Britain in 2017 by Hodder and Stoughton
This paperback edition published in 2018

A CIP catalogue record for this book
is available from the British Library.

ISBN: 978 1 444 92923 2

1 3 5 7 9 10 8 6 4 2

Printed and bound in China

Hodder Children's Books
An imprint of Hachette Children's Group
Part of Hodder and Stoughton
Carmelite House, 50 Victoria Embankment
London, EC4Y 0DZ

An Hachette UK Company
www.hachette.co.uk

www.hachettechildrens.co.uk